COTTONTAIL RABBIT : ALL FOUR FEET

A SNAKE CRAWL

CAT

FRONT PAW PRINT

DEER MOUSE

MY FOOTPRINT

Going
Barefoot

Going Barefoot

by *Aileen Fisher*

ILLUSTRATED BY ADRIENNE ADAMS

THOMAS Y. CROWELL COMPANY: *New York*

Going
Barefoot

How soon
how soon
is a morning in June,
a sunny morning or afternoon
in the wonderful month
of the Barefoot Moon?
I can go barefoot
like kittens and dogs,
bears and beetles
and hoppity frogs
as soon
as it's June!

March is too early
and May still cold—
not for my nose
but for toes,
I'm told.

Rabbits go barefoot
the whole year through.
If the sky is cloudy
or satiny blue
or puffy with wind
or fluffy with snow
or stuffy with heat,
away they go!
They never wear slippers
with straps or zippers,
they never wear shoes with laces,
they look very neat
(and they're certainly fleet)
when they hippity-hop
in their birthday feet
to hideaway rabbity places.

In grass, alas,
whenever they pass,
you can't see their footprints showing.
But over the snow
when they come and go
their tracks show Coming and Going.

How soon, how soon
is a bright before-noon
on a fair-footed, barefooted
morning in June?
I can go barefoot
just like a raccoon
in June!

April is rainy
and May still cold
under the new green grass,
I'm told,
for people like me,
but NOT for raccoons
who wear fur jackets and pantaloons.

RACCOONS!

Did you ever look
near a wildish brook
or a green-eyed pond
with a wood beyond
and see (on the bank
where the grass grows rank
and the mud is black)
a five-toed track?
Hands in front
and feet in back
like an all-four child
in a place so wild?
There a raccoon
on a late afternoon
or under the light
of a lantern moon
went looking for frogs
and mice to eat . . .
in his barefoot feet.
That's where he walked
in the thick black ooze
without any shoes.

And so will I
when the sun is high
in the wide June sky!

Bees
in trees,
ants
on plants,
frogs
in bogs,
cats
on mats,
wear
feet bare.

They wear them late
and they wear them soon,
they don't have to wait
for a day in June
to go barefoot.

Their toes are free
to squiggle and squish
wherever they be,
whenever they wish,
and if it's chilly
they just say, "Pish."
They don't have to wait
till it's summer-ish
like me!

Did you ever think
of the styles of shoes,
pair after pair,
that people wear?
Shoes with straps,
buckles and flaps,
low heels, high,
laces to tie . . .
oxfords, loafers,
boots, and sandals—
all kinds of shoes
that a shoe store handles.

Did you ever think
of the styles of feet
in the woods, on a path,
and beyond the street?
Feet that have paws
padded and thick,
feet that have claws
scratchy and quick,
horny feet,
thorny feet
(lasting for years),
hoppy feet,
kloppy feet,
hoofed . . . like a deer's.

Like a deer's!

Feet like a fawn's, a doe's, a buck's,
are sharp little feet
(not webbed like a duck's).
Sharp little hoofs of patent leather
walking through woods and fields together;
tracks on a trail with twists and turns,
tracks in the Opens
and lost in the ferns.

As soon
as soon
as the month is June,
the wonderful month of the Barefoot Moon,
I'll make some tracks myself!

Some things go barefoot
the whole year through.
But *I* don't go,
and neither do you,
though bees and beetles and spiders do.

Spiders are different
from just plain bugs
on ceilings and rugs.
Spiders have eight feet,
bugs just six . . .
but they're all
in a wonderful sort of fix:
running or sunning
or working or funning
they go around shunning
shoes!

The thread spiders spin
is sturdy and thin,
but they never make slippers
that feet slip in.
They string their lines
in pretty designs
between the rafters or ivy vines.

And so would I, too,
wouldn't you?

How soon, how soon
is a morning in June,
a barefoot morning or afternoon
when the sidewalk's warm
and the grass and clover
are green velvet carpets
that feet run over?

Down the hills,
along the valleys,
over the yards,
up the alleys,
making detours,
making sallies,
go dozens of feet
of mice and squirrels,
barefooted toes, barefooted heels
knowing how every Weather feels:

Tickle of grasses,
prickle of hay,
trickle of water along the way,
stickle of frost on a frosty day,
soft places, hard places,
be-on-your-guard places,
August, December, and May.

The tracks of squirrels
and the tracks of mice
are certainly nice
the way they go . . .
barefoot, you know.

You see them in winter
like neat little stitches,
crossing the woodlands,
the lawns and the ditches,
ducking through bushes
and stopping in niches.
(Squirrel tracks are bigger—
that's how you know which is.)

Neat little tracks
of thin little paws
with pink little pads
and sharp little claws,
show heel and toe
on the snow, you'll find,
daintily patterned and well-designed.
But think
how their feet
would make spattery sploshes
if they had on socks
and then shoes and galoshes . . .
like me and you
till winter is through
and spring comes to call
and the air turns blue
and the leaves are new
and birds back and all!

BIRDS!

How do birds sleep
in the maples and birches?

 By using the branches
for open-air perches.

Why don't they fall?
Aren't they taking big chances?

Not when their toes
make a clamp on the branches.

Small birds, tall birds,
old birds, bold birds,
new birds, bluebirds,
gay birds, jay birds,
strong birds, songbirds,
birds that sing and birds that cackle,
robin, chicken, goldfinch, grackle . . .
any bird that you can mention
doesn't have the least intention
of wearing shoes at any season.
And, you see, there is a reason:

Look at the linnet
swinging on a briar,
gone in a minute
to balance on a wire . . . .

Look at the flicker
jerking up a tree,
no one is quicker
at climbing than he. . . .

Look at the sparrow
hopping past a weed;
under the yarrow
he scratches up a seed. . . .

The duck on the river
take a look at him—
webbed feet quiver
and make him swim.

Birds? They are clever
but where would they be
if they ever, ever, ever
wore shoes like me?

How soon
how soon
is a day in June
when I won't wear shoes
on a bright forenoon,
won't wear moccasins,
won't wear sockasins,
only my feet—like kangaroos.

KANGAROOS!

Can you picture shoes
on KANGAROOS,
on those big long jumpity feet
they use?
Can you see them hopping
easily, lightly,
breezily, brightly,
wonderfully fleet
with *shoes* on their feet?

Some jump five feet,
some jump ten,
fifteen, twenty,
and then again
kangaroos—why, sakes alive—
have jumped as high as twenty-five!
But not in boots that cowboys use.
Only, of course,
in their "birthday" shoes.

They don't have to think
that March is early,
or April—when leaves
are young and curly,
or May—when everything's
green as clover.
They don't have to wait
till the rains are over.
They don't have to wait. . . .

How long do I?

"When is it June,
and then July?"
I ask my mother.
I ask, "How soon
does the calendar say
is the Barefoot Moon?"

My mother looks
and blinks her eyes,
the kind of blink
for a big surprise.
"The page that was May
is gone!" she cries.
"The month that was May is over.
So soon!
I guess we're beginning the Barefoot Moon.
It's June."

JUNE!

The day is warm
and a breeze is blowing,
the sky is blue
and its eye is glowing,
and everything's new
and green and growing. . . .

My shoes are off
and my socks are showing. . . .

My socks are off. . . .

Do you know how I'm going?

B A R E F O O T !

About the Author

AILEEN FISHER was born in Iron River, Michigan, in the Upper Peninsula. When she was five, the family moved to a farm outside Iron River, and it was there that she learned to love the outdoors, to know the many different kinds of animals and birds, and to look forward to the changing seasons.

Miss Fisher attended the University of Chicago and was graduated from the University of Missouri with a degree in journalism.

After working in Chicago for a few years, Miss Fisher moved to Colorado, near Boulder. She lives on a 200-acre ranch in the foothills with a view of the Arapahoe Peaks.

About the Illustrator

ADRIENNE ADAMS lives with her husband in an old stone and log house in New Jersey, on twenty-one acres of land. Their winters are spent in their small house in the Virgin Islands.

Miss Adams attended Stephens College and the University of Missouri. She came to New York to work in the field of fabrics, and became a display art director and a free-lance designer. The first book she illustrated, *Bag of Smoke*, was written by her husband, John Anderson. Miss Adams now devotes all of her time to illustrating.

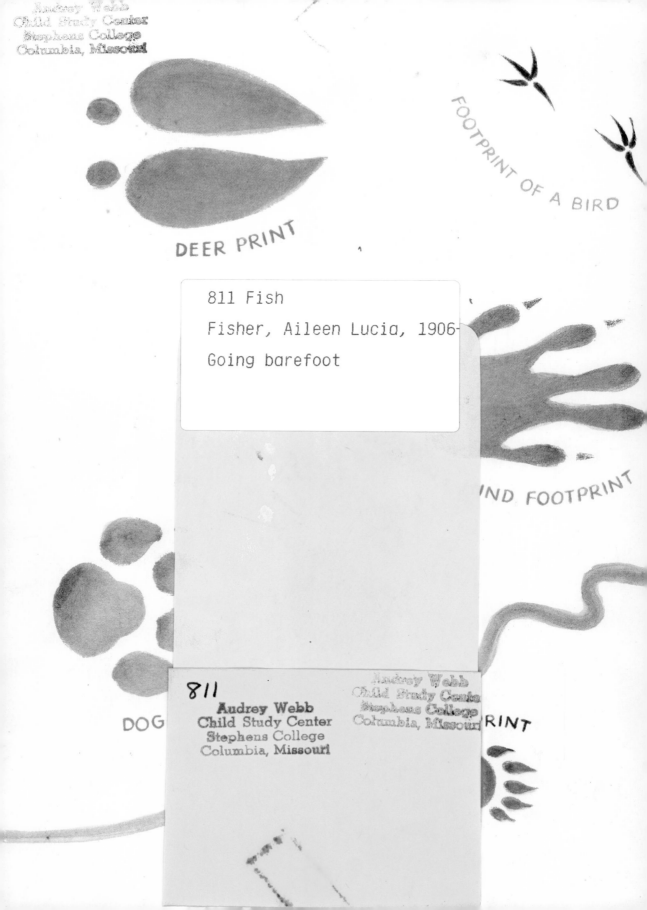

DEER PRINT

FOOTPRINT OF A BIRD

...IND FOOTPRINT

DOG...

...RINT

811 Fish

Fisher, Aileen Lucia, 1906-

Going barefoot